MISSING!

"Good as new," said Ranger Curtis. He looked down at Frank and frowned kindly. "Now, be careful in the park, Frank! I don't want to have to do this again anytime soon."

"Yes, sir," Frank said. He turned to Mrs. Ackerman. "Thanks, Mrs. Ackerman. Now can I go check on my bike?"

"Sure thing, Frank."

Before she was even finished speaking, Frank was off and running. Behind him, he heard Mrs. Ackerman yell, "And remember to be careful!"

Two minutes later Frank was back where his bike was. Or rather, where his bike used to be.

The ditch was empty.

THE **HARDY BOYS**®

SECRET FILES #6

 The Bicycle Thief

BY **FRANKLIN W. DIXON**

ILLUSTRATED BY **SCOTT BURROUGHS**

ALADDIN ▪ NEW YORK LONDON TORONTO SYDNEY

This book is a work of fiction. Any references to historical events, real people, or real locales are used fictitiously. Other names, characters, places, and incidents are the product of the author's imagination, and any resemblance to actual events or locales or persons, living or dead, is entirely coincidental.

✦ALADDIN

An imprint of Simon & Schuster Children's Publishing Division
1230 Avenue of the Americas, New York, NY 10020
First Aladdin paperback edition August 2011
Text copyright © 2011 by Simon & Schuster, Inc.
Illustrations copyright © 2011 by Scott Burroughs
All rights reserved, including the right of reproduction in whole or in part in any form.
ALADDIN is a trademark of Simon & Schuster, Inc., and related logo is a registered trademark of Simon & Schuster, Inc.
THE HARDY BOYS is a registered trademark of Simon & Schuster, Inc.
For information about special discounts for bulk purchases, please contact Simon & Schuster Special Sales at 1-866-506-1949 or business@simonandschuster.com.
The Simon & Schuster Speakers Bureau can bring authors to your live event. For more information or to book an event contact the Simon & Schuster Speakers Bureau at 1-866-248-3049 or visit our website at www.simonspeakers.com.
Designed by Lisa Vega
The text of this book was set in Garamond.
Manufactured in the United States of America 0711 OFF
10 9 8 7 6 5 4 3 2 1
Library of Congress Control Number 2010938942
ISBN 978-1-4169-9396-4
ISBN 978-1-4424-2644-3 (eBook)

◖ CONTENTS ◗

1 0

And They're Off!

The crowd was cheering so loudly, Joe could barely hear the announcer. It didn't matter. He knew when the announcer called his name, because the crowd started screaming, "Joe! Joe! Joe!"

Joe stuck one hand up in the air and waved to the hundreds of people who lined the streets of Bayport for the annual Junior Bike Rally. Frank did the same when his name was called. They were next to each other on the starting line. On either side of them were a dozen other kids they knew. Chet Morton and his sister Iola were on their left. On their right was Phil Cohen, Bayport Elementary's resident tech expert. But Frank and Joe ignored them all. They each knew that the biggest challenge would come from the other.

This was going to be a tough race. The track led all around town. They would ride on roads and on dirt paths through the woods. Although the roads

had been closed for the race, none of the racers knew the exact route they would take. Instead, they would have to look for little blue flags that would mark the path. This was going to be a challenge— and Frank and Joe were ready for it!

"Ready, little brother?" Frank asked.

Joe stuck out his tongue. He hated being called "little" anything. Especially since he was almost as tall as Frank (though he was a year younger).

Before Joe could respond, the race judge stepped out onto the track. The crowd grew quiet.

"On your mark!" the judge yelled. He pulled a white-and-black checkerboard handkerchief from his pocket. The racers readied themselves on their bikes.

"Get set!" He held the handkerchief high up in the air. All the racers stood up a little on their pedals, to give themselves an added push.

"Go!" the judge screamed. The crowd screamed with him. The noise was deafening. But the racers didn't notice. They had only one thing on their minds: winning.

"And they're off!" yelled the announcer.

Most of the racers stuck together at the start. They were a tight pack of bicycles, so close together that every turn threatened to knock the riders into one another. A few of the boys pulled ahead. Frank and Joe weren't worried about them. This was a long race. It required patience. Starting in first place didn't mean ending there. They stayed in the pack. Frank and Joe raced past the town hall, Bayport Elementary School, and even their own house. All along the streets of Bayport, people cheered as the racers rode by.

At the second mile, they came to the first difficult part of the race: a few hills right in a row. Joe and Frank made their way up and down the slopes, pedaling a little faster to get up those hills. All was fine until one of the racers in front of them missed a turn and crashed right in front of them!

Frank and Joe both pulled back on their handlebars and swerved just in time, right before they caused a bike pileup! Joe looked back to see if the other rider needed help, but someone was already on the way to help.

The race continued, with one fewer racer. The sun was hot and bright. The wind threw dirt from the road into their faces. But they kept going. They were already at the halfway mark. Now it was time to kick it into high gear.

Slowly Frank and Joe pulled ahead. They left

the pack of racers behind. One by one they passed the kids who had been out front. Soon it was as if they were the only people in the race. No one could touch them. Pedals flying, feet pumping, they raced in silence. The only sounds they made were their heavy breathing, or the occasional "Ooph!" as one of them hit a dip in the road.

They were neck and neck as they came to the end of the race.

Joe managed to get the inside position. For half a mile the boys rode next to each other, so close that Frank could have scratched an itch on Joe's hand. Ahead of them the finish line drew closer. Cheering crowds surrounded it on each side, waiting to see who would win, Frank or Joe Hardy.

POP!

Suddenly there was a loud explosion, like a balloon breaking.

"AAAAHHHHHHH!" Frank screamed.

 7

Joe looked ahead of him. There was the finish line. He looked back. Frank was gone. Joe stopped. The voices of the crowd faded. The finish line disappeared. The course behind them was the dirt path that led from the Hardy house down through Bayport Park, which was just outside downtown Bayport. But there was still no sign of Frank.

"Frank? Where are you?" Joe yelled.

"Over here," came a weak voice.

2

Crash!

Are you okay?"

Joe peered down into the ditch on the side of the road. Frank lay on his side, half under his bike. Frank shook his head. Slowly he got up.

"Yeah, I think so," he said.

"What happened?"

"My bike blew a tire!" Frank pointed to the front wheel of his bike. Sure enough, there was a nail in it. The tire was as flat as a pancake. There was no way he'd be riding any farther until they fixed it. Then Joe noticed something else.

"Uh, Frank?"

"Yeah, Joe?"

"Your arm—it's bleeding!"

Frank looked down at his arm. Joe was right. He had a long scratch running down his arm. It didn't look that deep, but it was definitely bleeding. And it definitely hurt!

"Ow!" said Frank. "I better clean that."

"Yeah," said Joe. "First we'll patch you up. Then we'll patch the bike."

As the other racers started crossing the finish line, Frank pulled his backpack off. In a minute they would have Frank's bike all fixed up—and Frank fixed up too!

Joe opened the backpack for the first aid kit. The bag also had water, sandwiches, a tire patch kit, a Frisbee, a notebook (for any clues they might come across), a baseball (both Frank and Joe were on the local Little League team, the Bayport Bandits), and a mitt.

Joe turned the backpack upside down and shook it. Out tumbled their mom's lunch, her extra sweater, a bottle of water, and her planner!

"Oh no!" said Frank. "I grabbed the wrong bag!"

The whole Hardy family had identical black bags, which their father had purchased for them years ago. This happened a lot. Joe had once had to make up show-and-tell from his Aunt Gertrude's knitting collection, and Mr. Hardy had once brought Frank's science project to an important meeting.

"We'll just have to go get the spare patch kit from the garage," said Joe. "Hopefully, Mom has some Band-Aids in here too!"

Joe picked up the water bottle. Frank rolled up his sleeve and held out his arm.

"Ready?" Joe said. Frank nodded.

Joe poured the clean water all over Frank's cut.

"Ouch!" said Frank. "That stings."

It may have stung, but the water did its job, washing out all the dirt that had gotten into his cut. Now that the wound was clean, Frank found a small first aid kit in a pocket of the bag. He dried his arm with a clean piece of gauze, then pulled out the Band-Aids. One by one he put them across his cut.

"Good as new," he said. "Now let's get my tire fixed! But it would take me forever to wheel the bike back, and I might damage the tire even more. And we don't have anything to lock them up with. So you'll have to go get the kit, and I'll wait here."

Joe nodded. He gathered up their mom's stuff and put it all back into her bag. Then he hopped onto his bike and headed home.

Frank sat down next to his bike to wait. It wouldn't take Joe that long. A little farther into the park there was a water fountain. Frank hated to leave his bike alone, but he'd be able to see it from the fountain. And he was pretty thirsty. He decided to go for it.

Halfway to the fountain a familiar dog came bounding over.

"Lucy!" he said. "Down!"

Lucy nearly knocked Frank to the ground, because she was so eager to lick his face. Lucy had once stolen a baseball mitt from one of the Bayport Bandits, but they'd become good friends anyway. Lucy had a long history of crime, but thanks to her owner, Mr. Mack, everything got returned eventually.

"I'm sorry, Frank. Lucy, come here!"

That was Mr. Mack, Lucy's owner. He couldn't keep up with Lucy when she was off her leash, but he was always close behind.

"Hi, Mr. Mack," Frank said, once Lucy had gotten off him.

"Hi, Frank," said Mr. Mack. Then he paused. "Oh no," he said. "What happened?" He pointed to Frank's arm.

"I fell off my bike," Frank explained. "I just finished patching up my cuts." He proudly showed off his Band-Aid skills.

"You boys better be careful on those bikes. You go pretty fast," Mr. Mack warned.

"Yes, sir," Frank said. But Mr. Mack was already moving away, running after Lucy. Frank started walking again.

"Hey, Frank! Over here! Frank! Frank! Over here! Come play with us! Fraaank!"

There was only one person in all of Bayport who could talk quite that fast. Cissy "Speedy" Zermeño was Bayport's fastest talker—and the fastest pitcher on the Bayport Bandits.

Speedy and a few of the other Bandits were playing catch right off the path, doing a little pre–Little League spring training. Before Frank could say anything, Speedy threw the ball his way.

"Ow!" Frank said as he caught the ball. He

hadn't thought about his cut, and it hurt to move his arm. He dropped the ball. Twisting his arm to catch the ball had pulled on the Band-Aids, and now some of them were flapping loose. They wouldn't re-stick, so Frank pulled them off and put them in his pocket.

"Oh, man! What happened? I'm sorry. Did I do that? Does it hurt?" Speedy ran over to Frank, her mouth moving as fast as her feet.

"No. I fell off my bike. I guess catching the ball hurt my arm."

Speedy scooped up the ball and tossed it to one of the other Bandits.

"You should join us when you're done," she said. Speedy looked around. "Hey, where's Joe? And where's your bike?"

"Joe went to get our patch kit. We have to finish our race first, but we'll join you when we're done. And my bike is in the ditch back there."

"Cool. See ya later!" With that, Speedy was off.

Frank finally made it to the water fountain. He carefully stuck his arm under the cold stream of water. It stung, but not as much as when Joe had cleaned it the first time.

"Ew!" came a voice from behind him. "What are you doing? Don't you have a shower at home?"

Frank turned around to find Adam Ackerman standing behind him. Adam was the town bully. He and Frank and Joe had gotten in each other's way before. Adam was just about the last person Frank wanted to see right then.

"I fell off my bike," Frank explained. He held out his arm to show the cut. "I was just washing—"

"Aw, are you going to cry?" Adam teased. "Waah! Waah!" he yelled. He balled his hands into fists and rubbed his eyes.

"Boys!" yelled Mrs. Ackerman, who had come

up behind them. "What is going on here? Why are
you making that noise?"

"I was just trying to help Frank, Mom!" said
Adam. "He was crying because he cut himself."

Adam grabbed Frank's arm and pulled it toward
his mother.

"Ow!" said Frank. Before he had a chance to correct Adam, Mrs. Ackerman had pulled Frank to her.

"My! That is a nasty cut. What happened?"

For what felt like the fiftieth time, Frank explained.

"I fell off my bike, Mrs. Ackerman. Joe went to get a patch kit because my tire was flat. I just wanted to get some water."

"Well, we're going to have to go to the park ranger's station. They'll fix you right up."

"But—my bike—I can't—" Frank tried to tell Mrs. Ackerman he couldn't leave his bike behind, but Mrs. Ackerman ignored him.

"Now, Adam, you stay here. With that hurt foot of yours, I don't want you walking any more than you have to."

She waggled her finger at Adam. Adam put

on his best innocent face and nodded. The week before, while chasing some younger kids on the playground at school, he had fallen and hurt his toe pretty badly. He could walk on it, but he was still limping a little. Frank couldn't help but think that it served him right.

Mrs. Ackerman dragged Frank to the park ranger's station, which was in the middle of Bayport Park, far from his bike.

It was probably a good thing she did. Curtis, the ranger on duty, took one look at Frank's arm and tsked.

"That's a nasty cut. Hold out your arm."

Curtis cleaned the cut, put some antibacterial cream on it, and re-bandaged it.

"Good as new," said Ranger Curtis. He looked down at Frank and frowned kindly. "Now, be careful in the park, Frank! I don't want to have to do this again anytime soon."

"Yes, sir," Frank said. He turned to Mrs. Ackerman. "Thanks, Mrs. Ackerman. Now can I go check on my bike?"

"Sure thing, Frank."

Before she was even finished speaking, Frank was off and running. Behind him, he heard Mrs. Ackerman yell, "And remember to be careful!"

Two minutes later Frank was back where his bike was. Or rather, where his bike used to be.

The ditch was empty.

3

Mix-up Fix-up

Joe pedaled back home as fast as he could. Within seconds he was back to daydreaming about winning. He could almost hear the crowd cheering his name.

"Joe! Joe, where are you going?"

It wasn't a crowd. It was his mother, leaning out the kitchen window. He had biked right past their house! Good thing she had been looking out the window at that moment.

He turned around and hopped off his bike. He ran inside at top speed.

His mom, dad, and aunt Gertrude were all sitting around the kitchen table, eating a late lunch.

"Slow down, Joe!" said Mr. Hardy.

Joe skidded to a halt.

"Sorry, Dad! Frank's bike blew a tire, and we brought Mom's bag by accident, so we couldn't fix it." Joe held up the black backpack.

"Not again," Mrs. Hardy groaned. "Fenton, we have to get new bags for the family. This is getting silly."

"But . . . they were on sale!"

Everyone laughed. Their father could never pass up a bargain.

"Well then, I'm sewing name tags on them. On the outside. Tonight!" Mrs. Hardy said.

Aunt Gertrude took the bag from Joe and

gave him the correct one, with all his bike supplies.

"Want a ride back to the park?" she asked.

"I'm cool!" yelled Joe. He was already running out the door.

"Be back by dinnertime!" his father yelled.

"Remember, sunset is your curfew, and your aunt Gertrude is making lasagna!"

This time Joe took a shortcut. Instead of following the rambling path all the way down to the park, he went straight through town. He knew if he took a left after the grocery store, and then a

right at the pharmacy, and then rode across Mrs. Ackerman's backyard, he'd be there in half the time it normally took.

Or was it a right after the grocery store and a left at the pharmacy? Or maybe they were both rights? Frank and Joe almost always biked on the path, since it was easier to race on the path. And he didn't go by Adam Ackerman's house very often. His shortcut turned into a very long cut! It had already taken him twice as long as his normal trip.

Gosh, this is hard! Joe thought. His legs were starting to hurt. *How do real bike racers do it?* he wondered.

Finally he found his way. It was a left at the grocery store and a left at the pharmacy! He rode carefully across the path in Mrs. Ackerman's backyard, avoiding her many flower beds. Frank's bike had already gotten a flat tire. Nothing else could go wrong today.

Bayport Park appeared in front of him. He rode back to where he'd left Frank and his bike. In a few minutes they'd have the tire patched. And then he could try to rejoin the race—and beat his brother, at least, if no one else!

Except, when he got back to the ditch, there was no Frank! There was no bike! Something in the back of Joe's mind began to tingle. This was starting to feel like a mystery. And if there were one thing Joe loved more than biking (and beating Frank in a race), it was solving mysteries.

Joe looked around. Luckily the ground in the ditch was still muddy and wet from recent rain. He could see clearly the place where Frank's bike had gone over the edge. The ground was all torn up where the bike had landed. And next to it he saw three sets of footprints. One was his, and the other was Frank's. There was also one he didn't recognize.

He knew his and Frank's footprints because he and Frank had carved distinctive patterns into their shoes, so that if one of them was ever lost, the other could find him. Joe's shoes had stars on them, and Frank's had dinosaurs. Their mom had gotten mad about it, because the first time they had done it, they had cut all the way through the soles! But they got it right the second time.

Today it had come in handy at last! Joe followed the track of dinosaurs up out of the ditch. They stopped at the road. Joe judged the angle. After a little looking, he was able to pick up the tracks on the other side of the path, in the park proper. He didn't make it far before Frank nearly ran straight into him.

"Joe!" yelled Frank. "Guess what?"

"Your bike was stolen," said Joe.

"How did you know?" Frank stared at him in shock. How did Joe know that?

4

The Six Ws

oe said nothing. He just smiled.

"How did you know someone took my bike?" asked Frank again.

"Say I'm the smartest."

Frank stuck his tongue out.

"Say it!"

"Fine," said Frank. "I'm the smartest." This time it was his turn to smile. "Now, how did you know?"

Joe laughed. He knew when he'd been beaten

fair and square. "Because you don't have it with you," he said. "And I followed your footprints out here, and there was no bike tread, which means you didn't bring it out here and then hide it."

Frank nodded. "Looks like we've got ourselves a case," he said. He wasn't happy that his bike was missing. He knew his parents were going to be upset if it was gone. It would cost money to replace it, and his piggy bank was low. The bike had been a birthday present. If he had lost it, he was going to be in a lot of trouble. It might take him months to be able to afford a new bike. But still, he couldn't keep the excitement out of his voice. If there were anything he liked better than biking, it was solving a mystery. And he was pretty sure he and Joe could figure this one out. They'd already solved more than one case.

Frank reached into his bag and pulled out a notebook and a pen. The boys sat beneath a big tree.

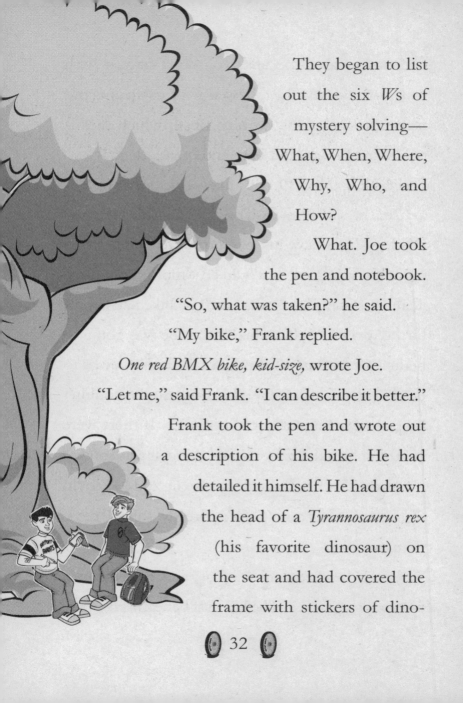

They began to list out the six *W*s of mystery solving—What, When, Where, Why, Who, and How?

What. Joe took the pen and notebook.

"So, what was taken?" he said.

"My bike," Frank replied.

One red BMX bike, kid-size, wrote Joe.

"Let me," said Frank. "I can describe it better."

Frank took the pen and wrote out a description of his bike. He had detailed it himself. He had drawn the head of a *Tyrannosaurus rex* (his favorite dinosaur) on the seat and had covered the frame with stickers of dinosaurs. Around the back wheel was painted the word "Bayport," and on the front was the word "Bandits." Frank and Joe had both painted their wheels for when the Bandits had won the local Little League championship and they'd been in the winner's parade. Finally, the handlebars had blue tassels on the ends. Not just because Frank liked how they looked, but also because the string often came in handy for fixing things or tying things together.

Once he'd finished describing the bike, he drew it—just in case they needed to make a "lost bike" poster.

No one else had a bike quite like his. Bayport was a small town. Anyone who saw it would know it was his.

When. "How long were you gone with Mrs. Ackerman?" Joe asked.

"Not very long. Maybe fifteen minutes."

Joe wrote down ~ *fifteen minutes*. Their mother had taught them that the symbol ~, or "tilde" as it was called, meant "about" or "almost." It was useful shorthand when taking notes on a case.

"That wasn't much time," said Joe. "Whoever took your bike made off with it fast."

Where. "Well, that one is easy," said Joe.

Bayport Park bike trail, he wrote in the notepad. He drew a large square to represent the park. Then he drew a curvy line for the bike trail. Finally he put an *X* where the bike had been.

Why. Joe wrote the word "why" in big letters. Then he stopped. For a moment both boys scratched their heads.

"Someone could have taken it to use themselves," said Joe. He wrote it down in the notebook.

"True," said Frank. "But they'd have to be my size. And it would be pretty obvious that it was my bike." He thought for a second. "Maybe they took it for the parts?"

Joe wrote down *Parts*.

"What if someone took it to get back at you?" said Joe. Not everyone was always happy with their mystery solving. They'd gotten more than one person in trouble in the past. Frank hated to think he had an enemy, but it was possible. He nodded. Joe wrote down *Enemy* in the notebook.

Who. This was the most important question.

"It had to be someone nearby," said Joe. "Think back. Who did you see?"

"I ran into Mr. Mack and Lucy!" said Frank. "And you know how Lucy is." Lucy was a great dog, but she had a habit of stealing things and burying them in the woods.

"A bike seems pretty heavy for Lucy to drag away," said Joe. "But who knows? And maybe Mr. Mack saw something."

He wrote them down in the notebook.

"Who else?" he asked.

"Well, I saw Speedy. I don't think she'd take my bike, but she's a witness. We should talk to her."

Cissy "Speedy" Zermeño, Joe wrote.

"Oh!" said Frank. "When Mrs. Ackerman took me to the ranger station, Adam stayed behind. And I'd told him that I'd fallen off my bike."

If anyone had reason to be mad at Frank, it was Adam. They'd caught him playing tricks on people a few times in the past. It would be just like him to steal Frank's bike.

Joe added his name to the list. "Cool," he said. "Is there anything else we should write down?"

Frank thought for a moment. He shook his head and jumped to his feet. "Nope! Let's get started."

"Right," said Joe. "But first I'm going to lock my bike up to a tree, now that we have your bag. I'd hate to lose both our bikes in one day!"

5

All Bark, No Bike

et's talk to Mr. Mack first," said Frank.

"But Adam's our best suspect," said Joe.

"Yeah, but Mr. Mack was the first person I saw. And we don't have any proof that Adam took my bike. Maybe Mr. Mack saw something. You know Dad says to get all the evidence first. And to start with the people who are going to be the most helpful. Besides, we don't know where Adam is."

"We don't know where Mr. Mack is either," said Joe.

"But it's easy to find him. Just follow the whistle!"

Mr. Mack was always whistling. He was a great whistler, and he could do just about any song he'd ever heard. Lucy liked to bark along with his whistling. They would be easy to find in the park.

Frank and Joe started off in the direction Frank had last seen Mr. Mack headed—running after Lucy toward the big lawn. The big lawn was at the center of Bayport Park. It was where people went to sit on picnic blankets and play Frisbee. There was a pond at the center, where dogs liked to drink. Sometimes they even swam in it.

"Running around and taking stuff is thirsty work," said Frank. "I bet Lucy was heading toward the pond."

Sure enough, Lucy was paddling around in the pond when the boys showed up. Mr. Mack was sitting on one of the benches, reading his paper.

"Hi, boys!" said Mr. Mack. "How's that arm, Frank?"

"Not bad," said Frank.

"That's good. Sorry I couldn't stop to help you earlier. She's been crazy today." He pointed toward Lucy, who was happily paddling back and forth in the water.

"It's okay. But maybe you can help us out now!" said Frank. He explained what had happened to his bike. He showed Mr. Mack the picture he had drawn of it.

"Oh no!" said Mr. Mack. "That's terrible. Who do you think took it?"

Frank looked at Joe. Joe looked at Frank. They both looked at Lucy. Neither wanted to be the one to say it.

"Well, sir . . . we thought maybe—," Frank started.

"Remember that time when Lucy took Jason

Prime's mitt?" Joe asked. Jason was the star player on the Bayport Bandits. Lucy had taken his mitt and buried it right before a big game.

"You don't think . . . Lucy?" said Mr. Mack. "I don't know, boys. A bike would be an awful heavy thing for her to drag around. But she has been off leash all day."

"Do you know where she's been hiding things?" asked Frank. Lucy always hid the stuff she stole somewhere in the woods.

"There's one way to find out." Mr. Mack pulled a chew toy shaped like a bumblebee out of his bag. "This is one of her favorite things to hide."

He threw the chew toy into the air. Lucy came racing out of the water and grabbed the toy before it hit the ground. Then she was off and running.

"Chase after her, boys! I'll do my best to keep up," yelled Mr. Mack. He didn't need to tell Frank and Joe twice.

Lucy raced through the big lawn. She was fast, but Frank and Joe were two of the best runners at Bayport Elementary School. Their father always told them that a good detective counted on his brain the most—but his legs were a close second!

If it had been a regular race, Frank and Joe would have been able to keep up with Lucy. But Lucy zigged and zagged. She ran through picnics and volleyball games. Frank and Joe had to run their hardest just to keep up with her.

"Sorry!" yelled Frank as he ran through a family's barbecue.

"Coming through!" yelled Joe as he interrupted a game of catch.

Slowly Mr. Mack's whistling faded into the background. When Frank looked back, he couldn't even see him anymore. If they lost Lucy now, they'd have to wait until she came back and start all over again!

Lucy loved taking stuff. But she also loved being chased! If it were possible for a dog to smile, Lucy would have had a huge smile across her face.

Finally, after running around the big lawn three times, Lucy ran into the woods.

"Careful!" yelled Frank. "We don't want to lose her now."

"Right!" yelled Joe. "And I'm going to try not to lose an eye, either."

It was hard to see Lucy through the trees. But they could still hear her running. Then, suddenly, the sound stopped. It was replaced by the sound of digging.

"She's burying the toy," said Joe. "But where is she?"

The boys looked around. There was no sign of Lucy. Then they saw dirt flying up into the air.

"There!" yelled Frank.

The boys ran over. She was sitting at the bottom of a deep hole, happily kicking dirt around. The hole was filled with things. Aside from Lucy's favorite toy, there were three tennis balls, two dolls, a book, two pairs of glasses, an empty backpack, and dozens of sticks.

But there was no sign of Frank's bike.

"Darn," said Frank. He hadn't really thought

Lucy had stolen his bike, but he'd gotten his hopes up anyway.

"Sorry, Frank," said Mr. Mack, who had just caught up with them. "So that's where my glasses went!" He began to pick all the important things out of the hole.

"It's okay," said Frank. "I'm glad she wasn't the one who took it."

"But," said Joe, "maybe she can help us find out who did take it?"

"We'd be happy to help you boys any way we can. But how?" asked Mr. Mack.

"Well, she's good at finding where she hid all of this stuff," said Joe. "So maybe she can track whoever took Frank's bike."

"Good idea!" said Frank.

Together Frank, Joe, Mr. Mack, and Lucy all headed back to the last place Frank had seen his bike.

"Okay, Lucy," said Frank. "I need you to find my bike. Can you do that, girl?"

Lucy whined and sniffed all around where the bike had been. She laid her ears flat against her skull. She put her nose low to the ground. Slowly she started walking away. Frank and Joe followed her down the path. Halfway through the park, she suddenly turned off the path, onto the dirt.

"Look," said Frank. He pointed to the ground. Lucy was following a set of footprints—and a bike track!

Lucy followed the tracks across the big lawn. But when they came to the road that ran through the center of the park, she lost them. The ground was drier here, and the tracks disappeared. They searched up and down, but neither the boys nor Lucy could find the trail again. They walked back to where they'd last seen the footprints. Frank kneeled down and drew them in his notebook.

"I'm sorry to get your hopes up, boys," said Mr. Mack when he caught up with them.

"It's okay, Mr. Mack," said Frank. "Lucy helped us more than you might guess. I think I know whose footprints these are!"

6

So Close and Yet So Far

I'll bet you anything those footprints belong to Adam Ackerman," said Frank.

"They're definitely the right size," said Joe. "But how can you be sure?"

"Look at the tracks," said Frank. "See how the left footprints are all deeper than the right ones? They were made by someone who couldn't step as hard on one side as the other. When Mrs. Ackerman took me to the ranger station, she told Adam to stay behind because he'd hurt his foot!"

"Let's find him!" said Joe.

That turned out to be easier said than done. Bayport Park was large, and Adam could have been anywhere. He might have even left the park already!

The boys decided to start their search where Lucy had lost the trail. They left the road behind and walked deeper into the park. Mr. Mack and Lucy followed behind them until Lucy grabbed a Frisbee and took off running.

"You boys keep going," said Mr. Mack. "We'll catch up."

The boys walked a little farther by themselves.

"Do you hear that?" said Joe.

"It sounds like little kids crying—and Adam Ackerman yelling," said Frank.

"Yup. Come on!"

They followed the sounds to the kids' playground. Adam was sitting on one of the swings, while two younger kids were sitting on the ground, crying.

"But it was our turn!" yelled one of them.

"Well, it's my turn now!" said Adam. "So beat it!"

The kids ran away, still crying.

"Very nice," said Joe. "Picking on little kids."

"Hi, Joe. Hi, Frank," said Adam. He looked very happy about something. And Frank was pretty sure he knew what it was.

"Okay, Adam, where is it?" said Frank.

"I have no idea where your bike is," said Adam. He pumped his legs and started to swing. The smile on his face grew bigger, until he swung too hard and made his foot throb.

Serves him right, Frank thought.

"If you don't know where my bike is," said Frank, "then how did you know that was what I was going to ask you about?"

"Lucky guess," Adam said.

 50

"We'll see about that!" said Frank. Right as Adam was at the top of his swing, Frank darted forward and grabbed his right shoe.

"Give that back!" yelled Adam.

"I will. In just one second," Frank said.

Joe took out the notebook, and Frank held the shoe up to the drawing he had made. It was a perfect match!

"I thought so!" said Frank. "You took my bike, and I want it back!"

"I'm not telling you anything," said Adam as he got off the swing.

Adam grabbed for his shoe, but Frank wouldn't let go.

"Give me my shoe!"

"Give me my bike!"

They went back and forth, each of them pulling as hard as they could. Suddenly a voice yelled from behind them.

"Boys! What is going on here?"

Adam and Frank both let go of the shoe at the same time. They went flying backward, landing on their backsides. It was all Joe could do to keep from laughing out loud.

"Nothing! We were just playing, Mom!" Adam's mother was standing at the edge of the playground, her hands on her hips, a suspicious look on her face.

"Adam took my bike—," Frank started to say.

But Adam cut him off. "I took Frank's bike

and moved it to a safe place!" he said quickly. "I saw he'd left it by the bike path, and I was afraid someone was going to steal it."

"Yeah," said Frank. "And I was just giving him his shoe so he could lead us to where he put it."

Adam's mother looked at the two of them. Frank put his arm around Adam's shoulder. They both tried to look innocent.

Adam's mother smiled. "Well," she said, "how nice of you boys to help each other out! Okay, then, let's all go get Frank's bike."

At that moment Mr. Mack and Lucy caught up with them.

"Did you find your bike?" Mr. Mack asked.

"We're on our way to get it!" said Mrs. Ackerman.

"Great," said Mr. Mack. "Let's go!"

Adam grumbled under his breath. He didn't seem happy to have to give Frank's bike back, especially because he had to do it in front of so many people. But it was better than getting in trouble with his mother.

As they walked Frank elbowed Joe and pointed to Adam's right leg. Sure enough, he was limping a little bit.

Adam led them back to the road where Lucy had lost the track originally. He kept walking down the road. They passed people picnicking and passed the ranger's station. They walked all the way to the statue of Bayport's founding fathers and mothers. Adam turned off the road at the memorial.

There was a small man-made pond and stream near the memorial. Frank and Joe often came here to throw the remains of their sandwiches to the ducks. On the bank of the river were a number of huge old willow trees. Their branches hung all the way to the ground. Adam walked over to the largest one.

"I put it under here for safekeeping," he said.

"More like he put it there so you would never find it!" Joe whispered to Frank.

Adam's mother beamed with pride. No matter how many times Adam got in trouble, she was convinced he was the best kid at Bayport Elementary School.

Adam pulled aside the branches of the willow tree to reveal a hidden patch of ground, just big enough for Frank's bike. There was only one problem.

The bike wasn't there.

7

Teamwork

What!" yelled Adam. "Where did it go?"

Adam swung his head back and forth, as though the bike might be hiding somewhere.

"Very funny," said Frank. "Now, where is my bike?"

"I left it here. I swear I did! You've got to believe me."

Adam's mother put her hands on her hips. She frowned. "Adam, sweetie. This is no time for games. You've had your joke. Now give Frank his bike."

"No, I'm not kidding, Mom!"

Adam beat around the tree branches, but the bike wasn't hiding anywhere.

"Adam, this is not funny. You had better find that boy's bike!" said Adam's mom. She didn't sound happy. The two of them began to argue. Frank looked around sadly.

"Did you get your bike, Frank?" Mr. Mack called out. Lucy came bounding into the space beneath the willow tree, someone's magazine in her mouth.

"Adam says he left it right here, but . . ." Frank looked around him. It was clear that his bike wasn't there.

"Well, maybe he got confused about which tree he left it under. There are a bunch of willows here, and they all look pretty similar."

"That's a smart idea, Mr. Mack!" said Joe. "Frank, you look through the trees to the left. I'll look through the ones to the right."

Frank and Joe looked under every willow tree in the area, even the ones that were way too small to hide a bike under. But Frank's bike was nowhere to be found.

"Do you think he's telling the truth?" Joe asked Frank.

Frank thought for a moment. "Yeah," he said. "I don't think he'd lie to his mom. And he seemed really surprised when my bike wasn't there."

"That can mean only one thing."

"Someone else must have stolen it from here!"

That meant they were back at the beginning! Or worse. Now they didn't have any real suspects. Both Lucy and Adam were now innocent. Who else could it be? There was only one thing to do.

It was time to look for more clues!

"We need to hurry," said Frank. The sun was getting lower in the sky. Soon it would be dark. He and Joe weren't allowed to be out alone after sunset. Frank was starting to worry.

"First we need to make sure Adam was telling the truth," said Joe.

The boys started to search outside the willow tree. If Adam really had hidden the bike beneath the tree, there would be—

"Tracks!" yelled Frank. Sure enough, there were more of Adam's footprints, with Frank's bike's tire track right next to them. They led under the tree, where Adam was still arguing with his mom. Mr. Mack and Lucy were still there too, hunting for a smell that Lucy could follow.

There was also a set of tracks that showed Adam walking out *without* Frank's bike.

"Look at these," said Joe.

Next to Adam's prints the ground was all torn

up. It looked as though a lot of people had walked through recently.

"Someone else was here!" said Joe.

"Yeah," said Frank sadly. "Lots of someones. Way too many to get any prints."

Joe looked closer. Frank was right. The ground was too much of a mess to get any individual footprint.

"Hey, guys! Looking for something?" Cissy had shown up behind them while they were searching.

"Yeah," said Joe. "Frank's bike."

Frank plopped down onto the ground. "We're never going to find it!" he said. "I'm going to be in so much trouble. We thought Adam had taken it, but he says he left it here. And now it's gone again!"

"He did leave it here," said Cissy. She grinned.

Frank jumped up. "How do you know that?" he asked.

"Easy," Cissy said. "I saw him!"

"You did?" said Frank. "Then, did you see who took my bike?"

"Yup," said Cissy. "It was me!"

"What?"

"A couple of us Bandits were practicing over on the big lawn, and we lost a ball, and I went after it. I saw Adam sneaking around with your bike. I could tell it was your bike, Frank, because no one else has a bike like yours. So I followed him here. I learned a few things from watching you guys solve crimes! When he left, I got the rest of the Bandits, and we picked up your bike and carried it away to safety. Then I went to go find you, but you were gone! I've been looking for you ever since."

Cissy stopped because she was out of breath. When she was excited, she talked even faster than usual.

"Did you hear that, Mom?" Adam yelled from under the willow. "I told you I was telling the truth!"

Frank looked at the ground. So that's why there were so many tracks! It was his teammates, rescuing his bike.

"You guys are the best!" he said. "So where is my bike now?"

"Follow me," said Cissy.

 63

She took off running. The only things faster than Cissy's mouth were her legs—and her pitching arm! Behind her came Frank and Joe. Behind them were Adam and his mom. And behind *them* were Mr. Mack and Lucy.

Two minutes later they were surrounded by the rest of the Bandits, who were playing a game of baseball.

"Hi, Frank! Hi, Joe!" everyone yelled.

"Hey, guys!" they yelled back.

"Hey, Frank. Your bike is right over here!" Cissy led them over to a big old oak tree. They walked around to the other side of it.

And there was nothing there.

"What?" said Cissy. "I left it standing right here!"

8

Missing in Action

"O h no," said Frank. "Not again!"

"I put it right here," said Cissy. "I swear!"

"I believe you," said Frank. "But I'm beginning to think my bike is cursed. Or else I am!"

The Bandits were putting away their baseball mitts and bats. Everyone was getting ready to leave. The sky was growing dark. Soon it would be nighttime, and Frank and Joe would have to go home. And then Frank was going to be in a lot of trouble.

"Maybe it's time to give up," Frank said. "My bike is gone."

"No way!" said Joe.

"Hey, everybody!" Joe yelled. The Bandits stopped putting their things away. Adam and his mom stopped arguing. Adam's little sister, Mina, came running over to listen. Mr. Mack stopped whistling. Even Lucy stopped barking to listen. "Frank's bike is missing! We've only got a little while before the park closes. Will you help us find it?"

"Yeah!" yelled everybody, except for Lucy, who barked.

"Great!" yelled Joe. "Let's team up and start looking. Everyone go in a different direction. The last place anyone saw the bike was over there by the big oak tree. Let's do it!"

Soon everyone was searching for Frank's bike. They were looking behind trees and under benches. They were looking down in every ditch and up on every hill.

"Wow," said Frank. "You guys are the best!"

"You've helped solve mysteries for everyone in town," said Cissy. "Now it's our turn to help you!"

They searched and searched and searched. They found two missing library books, a baby stroller, a bright red toy fire truck, an abandoned picnic basket, three sets of keys, and a cell phone. They found every baseball the Bandits had lost in every practice game in the last year. They found pretty much everything anyone had ever lost in Bayport Park.

But they didn't find Frank's bike.

Then a yell came up from the other side of the big lawn.

"I found it! I found it!" Jason Prime was jumping up and down and yelling. Frank came running over. Finally he was going to get his bike back.

Jason brought him to a bunch of trees on

the other side of the park. Frank could just make out a bicycle wheel peeking out from behind the branches.

"My bike!" Frank yelled. He ran around the trees. He was so excited to get his bike back.

But it wasn't his bike.

It was someone else's red bike. Frank's heart sank.

"I'm sorry," said Jason. "I thought it was your bike."

"It's all right," said Frank. He walked back across the big lawn, hoping someone else might have found his bike while he was gone. But no one had.

"I give up!" he cried. He sat down with his back against a tree. He stared out at the field, where all his friends were still searching. "My bike is . . ." He trailed off into silence. He had a weird look on his face.

"Your bike is what?" asked Joe.

But Frank ignored him. "Joe!" he said. "Look at that sign!"

Frank pointed at a sign on a tree above Joe's head. In big letters, it said: NO LITTERING— ENFORCED BY PARK RANGERS. ABANDONED PROPERTY WILL BE REMOVED.

A lightbulb went off in Frank's head. "What if

someone saw my bike and thought it had been abandoned?" he said to Joe.

"They would have gone and gotten the park ranger," said Joe.

"Right," said Frank. "And the ranger would have taken my bike away to the lost and found!"

"We've got to get to the park ranger's station before the park closes!"

And with that, Frank and Joe were up and running.

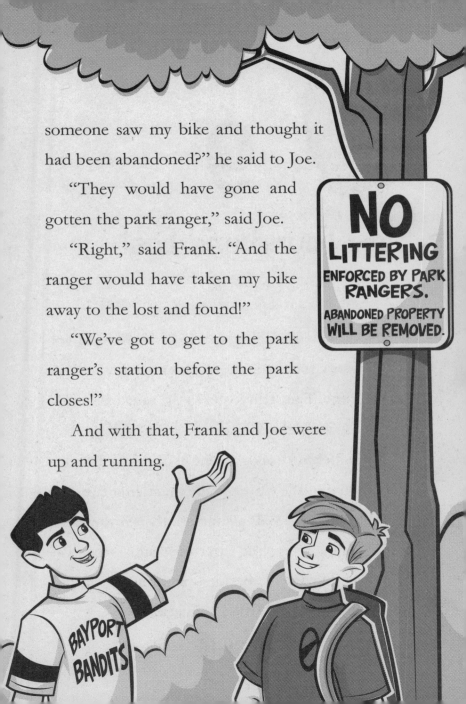

NO LITTERING ENFORCED BY PARK RANGERS. ABANDONED PROPERTY WILL BE REMOVED.

BAYPORT BANDITS

9

Found and Lost

The sun had almost set. If Frank and Joe were too late, the park ranger would be gone. They had to get to the ranger's station before the park closed!

Right behind was the entire Bayport Bandits team. Some of the players were practicing running and throwing the ball to one another at the same time. Cissy was juggling three baseballs—that was her other big talent, besides pitching the fastest fastball in the local Little League.

Behind the Bandits were Adam, his mom, and Mina. Mina was practicing with her hula hoop while she ran.

Behind the Ackermans were Mr. Mack and Lucy. Lucy kept darting forward to try to steal the baseballs from Cissy and the rest of the Bandits.

"Is this a parade?" asked two girls as Frank and Joe ran past them. They were packing up their stuff and getting ready to leave the park for the night. They had been blowing bubbles. When no one answered them, they grabbed their bubbles and joined the long line of people running through the park.

Next everyone ran by three musicians practicing in the park—a tuba player, a trumpet player, and a saxophone player. They took one look at everyone, picked up all their instruments, and started running behind the rest of the crowd.

Now there was a juggler, a hula-hooper, two bubble blowers, *and* a band following Frank and Joe. It really did look like a strange parade running through the park.

They ran across the big lawn and down past the Bayport memorial. They ran through the woods where Lucy buried her treasures, and near the willow trees where Adam had hidden Frank's bike. Finally they

made it to the ranger's station. Ranger Curtis was standing outside with a big trash bag, picking up the litter that people had left in the park throughout the day.

"Hey, what's going on here?" asked Ranger Curtis.

Frank opened his mouth to explain—but he was too out of breath from running to answer!

"It's a parade!" yelled one of the girls with the bubble wands. The musicians played a loud fanfare.

"A parade?" said Ranger Curtis. "I don't think we have that on the schedule! Do you have a permit for this?"

"No!" said Frank.

"No permit?" said Ranger Curtis. "Well, then, I'm afraid we simply can't have a parade. It's against the park rules."

"No, it's not that we don't have a permit!" said Frank, trying to explain.

"So you do have a permit?" said Ranger Curtis. Now he looked confused.

"No! We're not a parade."

"Well, you look like a parade," said Ranger Curtis, scratching his head and looking even more confused. "I've got the papers for a parade permit right here."

Ranger Curtis pulled a notebook from his pocket. "Now, let me just find them."

"We don't want to have a parade, Ranger Curtis!" said Frank. "We just want to find my bike. They're all helping me look for it."

"Oh," said Ranger Curtis. "Why didn't you say that in the first place?"

"I tried but—" Frank started to explain, but Ranger Curtis cut him off.

"This missing bike, what does it look like?"

Frank pulled out his notebook. He flipped to the page where he had drawn his bike. He held it out to Ranger Curtis.

"It looks like this, Ranger Curtis. Only it's red, not black and white."

"Oh, sure," said Ranger Curtis. "I know that bike. I found it all by itself in the middle of the park. You shouldn't have left it like that. It could have been stolen."

"That was my fault," said Cissy. "I was trying to give it back to him."

Frank thought about trying to explain all the places his bike had been that day. But it was just too much.

"Please, Ranger Curtis. I have to be home before dark. Is my bike here?"

Ranger Curtis smiled. "Sure is, son. I put it

on the other side of the ranger station for safe-keeping. Let's go get it and give this parade something to really celebrate!"

"Yay!" the whole crowd cheered. Finally they had found Frank's bike.

The musicians played their instruments. Cissy juggled. The girls blew

bubbles. Mina hula-hooped. The crowd celebrated and danced. They walked around the ranger's station.

And Frank's bike wasn't there.

The parade stopped. The music stopped. The bubbles stopped. The hula-hooping and juggling stopped.

"Where did it go?" asked Ranger Curtis. "You aren't playing a trick on me, are you, Frank?"

"No, sir! But it seems like someone is playing a trick on me. I can't find my bike anywhere."

"I don't know what to tell you, Frank. The bike was here just a few minutes ago. But it's time for me to close the park up. You'll have to come back and look for it tomorrow."

Frank sighed. There was nothing he could do. They'd have to go home without his bike.

10

Home Sweet Home

One by one everyone told Frank how sorry they were that they couldn't help him find his bike. Finally the only people left with Frank were Adam and his family, Cissy, and Joe. Adam came up to Frank.

"I'm sorry I took your bike," he said. He dug his toe into the dirt. "But I was going to give it back to you! I promise."

"I believe you," said Frank. "And this isn't your fault. But you shouldn't have taken it anyway."

"I know. I'll . . . I'll help you look tomorrow!" For the first time ever Adam Ackerman actually looked like he might cry.

"Thanks," Frank said. He held out his hand. They shook.

Adam and his family left.

"Hey, Frank!" Cissy said. "I know. We can make missing posters for your bike! I got some new colored pencils, and I can bring them over tomorrow after school, and then we can put posters all around Bayport! I'm sure someone knows where your bike is."

"Yeah," said Frank. "That sounds like a good idea." He tried to smile, but his heart wasn't in it.

Cissy gave him a hug. "See you tomorrow," she said. Frank and Joe said good-bye.

"I guess we should go get your bike and go home," Frank said to Joe.

Together, Frank and Joe went and unlocked

Joe's bike. Then they began the long walk home. Neither of them had won the 2011 Bayport Junior Bike Rally, Frank's arm was all scraped up, and worst of all, his bike was still missing. This was the worst day ever at the park.

Walking home seemed to take forever. It was so much quicker to ride a bike! In his head Frank did some math.

"Six months!" he suddenly said out loud.

"Six months what?" said Joe.

"That's how long it'll take me to save enough allowance money to buy a bike."

Six months without any more bike races. Six months without being able to bike to school or to the playground or to the store. Joe thought about it.

"I can lend you everything I have saved!" said Joe.

"Oh, wow! Thanks! How much is that?" asked Frank.

"Uh . . ." Joe pulled his pockets inside out. "Two dollars, seventy-three cents, some lint, and two sticks of gum?"

Frank sighed. It was going to be six months before he had a bike again.

The sun had just set when the Hardy house appeared down the street. In the flickering glow of the streetlights, Frank couldn't believe his eyes. He stopped. He stared. He rubbed his face and then looked again. He closed his eyes, counted to ten, and looked one more time.

"Frank . . . are you okay?" Joe asked.

"No," said Frank. "I've gone crazy. I'm pretty sure I'm seeing things. There's my bike!"

Frank pointed to the porch. Sure enough, a small red bike was leaning against the railing, all chained up.

"How is that possible?" asked Joe.

"I don't know!" said Frank.

 83

He ran over and inspected the bike. It was definitely his, from the dinosaur stickers on the frame to the words "Bayport Bandits" on the wheels!

"It's a miracle!" Frank said.

"Oh, hi, boys!" Aunt Gertrude opened the front door. "I was wondering when you would get home."

"Aunt Gertrude!" Frank and Joe yelled at the same time.

"Hey, Aunt Gertrude," said Frank, "do you know how my bike got here?"

"Sure do, Frank. I put it there."

"You put it there?"

How is that possible? Frank wondered. Had his Aunt Gertrude stolen his bike?

"After Joe came and got the patch, we expected you home pretty quickly. So when it started to get dark, I got worried. I drove down to the park, but I couldn't find you boys anywhere. Then, just as I was about to leave, I saw your bike sitting unattended by the ranger's station! I was worried someone might steal it, so I picked it up, threw it into the back of my car, and brought it home."

After all that, the bike was at his own house! Frank couldn't help but laugh.

Joe looked at the bike, and then looked at Frank. "The 2011 Bayport Junior Bike Rally rematch, tomorrow!"

"You're on!" said Frank. Then he looked up at Aunt Gertrude.

"Thank you, Aunt Gertrude!"

Frank rushed up the stairs and gave Aunt Gertrude a big hug.